KT-552-042

3 8003 03226 0515

Cumbria

First published in 2006 by
Franklin Watts
338 Euston Road
London
NW1 3BH

Franklin Watts Australia
Hachette Children's Books
Level 17/207 Kent Street
Sydney
NSW 2000

A CIP catalogue record for this book is available from the British Library.

ISBN 0 7496 6562 9 (hbk)
ISBN 0 7496 6568 8 (pbk)

Series Editor: Jackie Hamley
Series Advisors: Dr Barrie Wade, Dr Hilary Minns
Design: Peter Scoulding

Printed in China

Who's at the Zoo?

Written by
Ann Bryant

Illustrated by
Mike Phillips

W
FRANKLIN WATTS
LONDON • SYDNEY

Ann Bryant

"I wrote this story while I was in Africa travelling along bumpy roads in a jeep. I read it out to the hippos and elephants, but I'm not sure if they understood!"

Mike Phillips

"I live with my wife and my three children, along with one dog, two cats, three rabbits and 24 tropical fish. I feel like I live in my own little zoo!"

This is the day that I went to the zoo
with my mum and my dad
and my great granny Pru ...

... and with Becky, my sister,
and my best mate, Stu.

"Poor zebras," said Becky,
"they're plain black and white.
It can't be much fun
being half dark, half light.
I wish I could paint them
and make them look bright."

-ZEBRAS-
ZEBEDEE and
ZARA

"Those monkeys are making
a terrible din!
And look at their tails,
they're so spindly and thin.
Hey, Zac, take a photo,
and make sure I'm in."

Stu laughed at the hippos.
"They're so muddy, Zac!
All over their heads and their legs
and their backs.
And it's dried in the sun,
see, it's starting to crack!"

"Those elephants' ears are like
big leather bags.
And look at their skin!
It's all crinkles and crags.
It's weird how it wrinkles
and creases and sags."

"His backside's so bright!"
said Dad, chuckling away.
"Blue bottom for anyone?
What do you say?"
"No thank you!" we all said.
"Not likely! No way!"

Mum frowned at the lion
as she stared at his mane.
"I'm wondering if that goes
flat in the rain."
Great Granny said, "Hmm,
I should think it's a pain."

But little did Stu and the family know
that the animals, too,
were enjoying the show.
Watching these humans
is such fun, you know!

"Just stripes on the tummy?"
the small zebra said.
"Most odd!" said the big zebra,
nodding his head.
"And Zebedee, guess what?
They come off in bed!"

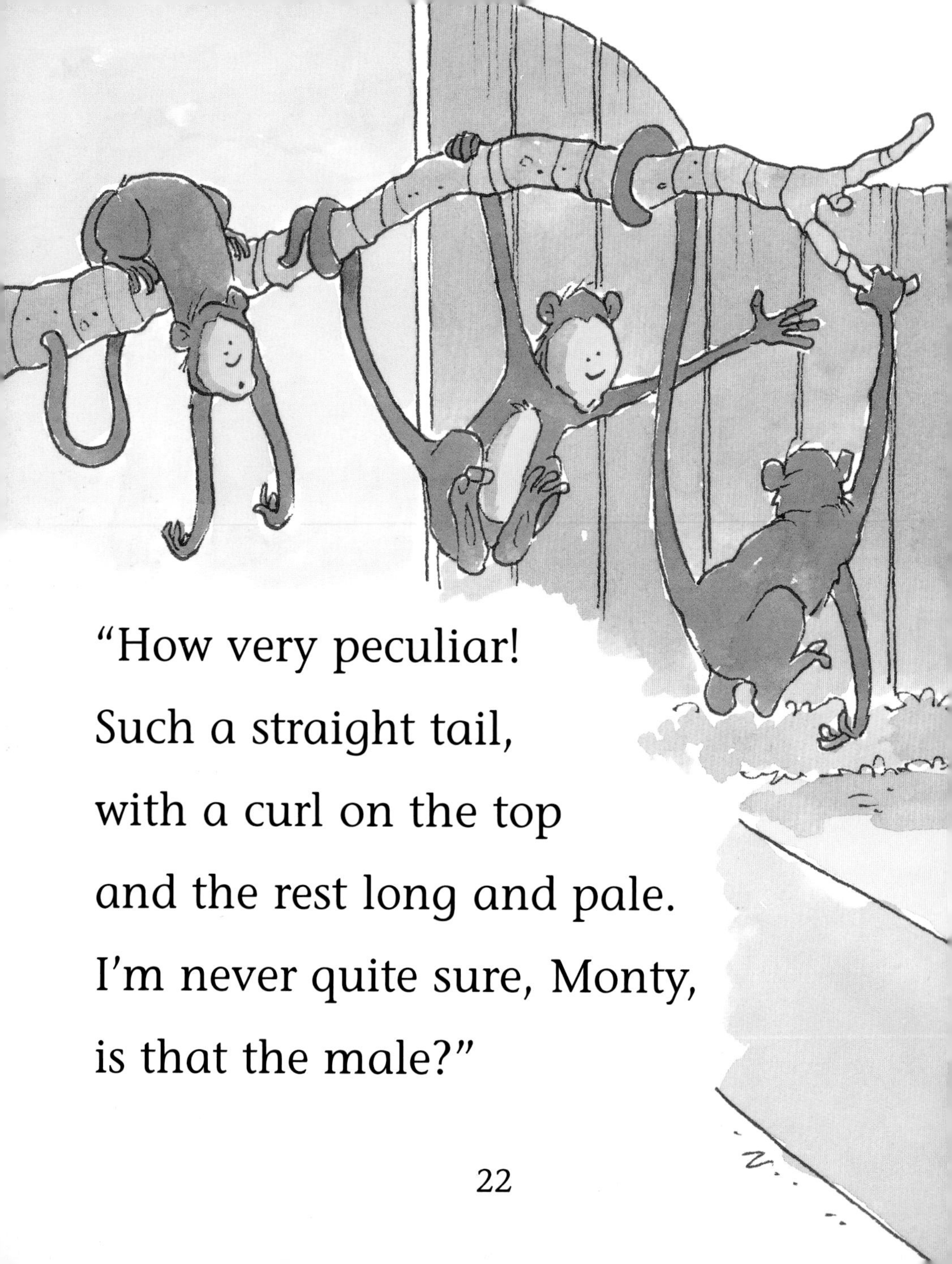

“How very peculiar!
Such a straight tail,
with a curl on the top
and the rest long and pale.
I’m never quite sure, Monty,
is that the male?”

"Well that boy's pathetic!
He's not even tried!
Rolling around should be done
with great pride.
You need mud all over,
not just on one side!"

"Those ears make me laugh.
What a strange way to grow!
Attached at the top and
like string beans below.
Don't stare at him, Ellie.
Just trumpet hello!"

"Look, Babs! On his head!
No it just can't be true.
It's such a strange place to
be coloured bright blue.
I bet that he's terribly
jealous of you!"

"My goodness, how odd!
Does she live in that nest?
No wonder she's looking
so terribly stressed.
Come on, Leo, darling,
let's go for a rest."

EXIT

Notes for parents and teachers

READING CORNER has been structured to provide maximum support for new readers. The stories may be used by adults for sharing with young children. Primarily, however, the stories are designed for newly independent readers, whether they are reading these books in bed at night, or in the reading corner at school or in the library.

Starting to read alone can be a daunting prospect. READING CORNER helps by providing visual support and repeating words and phrases, while making reading enjoyable. These books will develop confidence in the new reader, and encourage a love of reading that will last a lifetime!

If you are reading this book with a child, here are a few tips:

1. Make reading fun! Choose a time to read when you and the child are relaxed and have time to share the story.

2. Encourage children to reread the story, and to retell the story in their own words, using the illustrations to remind them what has happened.

3. Give praise! Remember that small mistakes need not always be corrected.

READING CORNER covers three grades of early reading ability, with three levels at each grade. Each level has a certain number of words per story, indicated by the number of bars on the spine of the book, to allow you to choose the right book for a young reader:

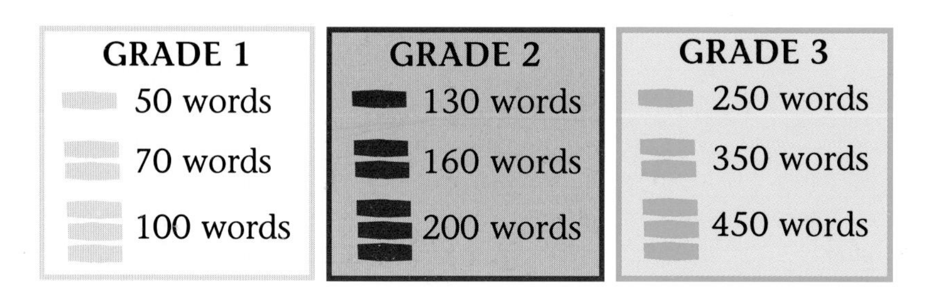

GRADE 1	GRADE 2	GRADE 3
50 words	130 words	250 words
70 words	160 words	350 words
100 words	200 words	450 words